W9-BWU-171

BONZINI!
THE TATTOOED MAN

STORY BY JEFFREY ALLEN
ILLUSTRATIONS BY JAMES MARSHALL

LITTLE, BROWN AND COMPANY

BOSTON   TORONTO

For My Brother Art

J. A.

For Edward Gorey

J. M.

TEXT COPYRIGHT © 1976 BY JEFFREY ALLEN
ILLUSTRATIONS COPYRIGHT © 1976 BY JAMES MARSHALL

ALL RIGHTS RESERVED. NO PART OF THIS BOOK MAY BE REPRODUCED IN ANY FORM
OR BY ANY ELECTRONIC OR MECHANICAL MEANS INCLUDING INFORMATION STORAGE
AND RETRIEVAL SYSTEMS WITHOUT PERMISSION IN WRITING FROM THE PUBLISHER,
EXCEPT BY A REVIEWER WHO MAY QUOTE BRIEF PASSAGES IN A REVIEW.

FIRST EDITION

T 09/76

Library of Congress Cataloging in Publication Data

Allen, Jeffrey.
  Bonzini! The tattooed man.

    SUMMARY: The children of a quiet Texas town have
their lives brightened by a tattooed man from a circus.
    [1. Tattooing – Fiction]   I. Marshall, James,
1942–   II. Title.
PZ7.A4272Bo   [E]   76-16537
ISBN 0-316-03427-4

Published simultaneously in Canada
by Little, Brown & Company (Canada) Limited

PRINTED IN THE UNITED STATES OF AMERICA

Kazoo, Texas, was hot and it was dull.

It was so hot you could sizzle a steak on a saddle.

And it was so dull that the only fun kids ever had was
chasing tumbleweeds and climbing the old, rusty water tower.

Then one day something happened!

A. W. Scroggins spotted a cloud of dust inching toward town.

"Someone's coming to Kazoo!" A. W. shouted to the others.

Everyone stopped chasing tumbleweeds to take a look.

"Someone's coming to Kazoo!"

Soon a brightly painted wagon rolled into town.

It was driven by the oddest looking man the children had

ever seen.

He was as tall as the sky and as bald as a berry.

His moustache was as long as a steer's horns, and

his hands were big enough to hold ten tumbleweeds each!

"Greetings, little ones!" the stranger bellowed as he leaped

from the wagon. "A sandstorm forced me off the trail to the

circus, and my mule is too tired to go another step."

"Circus?" A. W. asked. "You mean the kind with lions and clowns?"

"Dancing bears and elephants, too," the man answered.

"And I am Bonzini, The Tattooed Man, The Human Picture Show, Marvel of the Modern World, Feature Attraction!" With that, his big thumbs lifted the suspenders off his broad shoulders.

He removed his shirt and trousers, and revealed a dazzling display of pictures from neck to ankle.

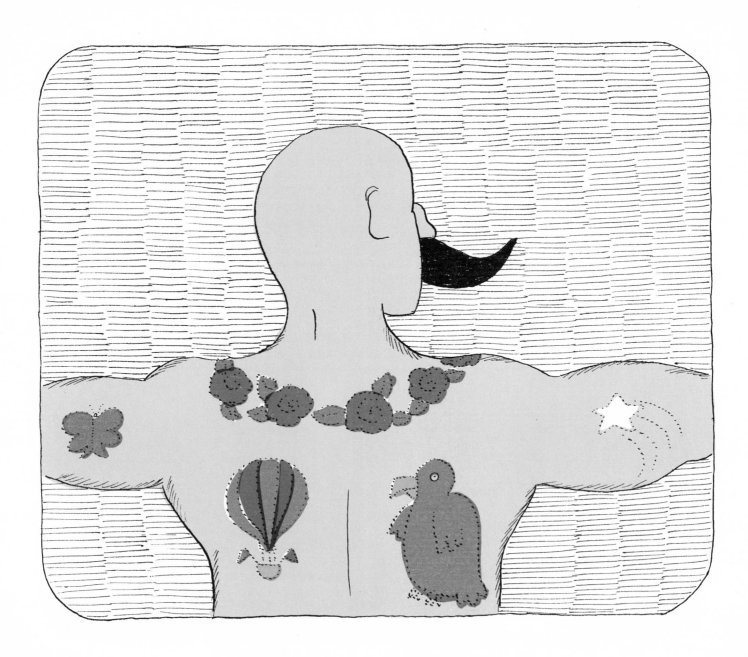

As Bonzini turned slowly 'round and 'round, the children stared in awe and became lost in the pictures on his body.

A. W. rode a camel.

He climbed a pyramid.

He floated down the Nile on a barge driven by one hundred
golden oars.

He charmed a snake in the cool shade of a date palm.

And he sipped lemonade on the throne of King Ramses.

The Tattooed Man suddenly clapped his hands.

The show was over as quickly as it had begun.

Everyone cheered loudly, and then sat down with Bonzini

beside a cactus.

It was quiet again, except for the sound of clothes

and sheets flapping in the gusty wind to dry.

Bonzini looked worried.

"What's the matter?" the children asked.

"How will a tired old mule get me back to the circus?" Bonzini wondered.

"Why can't you stay in Kazoo with us?" they answered.

"Because there will be a lot of disappointed children if I don't appear," he explained.

The kids decided they would help Bonzini.

His show was too good to miss.

Everyone thought long and hard.

What could they do?

"I have an idea!" A. W. exclaimed.

So with hammers and nails, ropes and poles, they turned the flapping sheets into giant sails, and hoisted them atop Bonzini's wagon.

The wind that blew the tumbleweeds puffed the sails.

Bonzini was slowly on his way.

The wind blew harder, the wagon rolled faster, and A. W.,
afraid Bonzini might never return, ran after him.
"Bonzini! Wait for me! Please take me with you!"

But the wind howled, and Bonzini yelled back,

"I can't wait! I can't stop the wind!"

A. W. ran back to town, and climbed the water tower. He saw
Bonzini's wagon grow smaller and smaller until it finally
disappeared.

A. W. felt sad, and wondered if Bonzini, The Tattooed Man,
The Human Picture Show, Marvel of the Modern World,
Feature Attraction, would ever return.

A. W. stayed on the water tower to watch.

"Come down and chase tumbleweeds with us!"

the others begged. "He'll never come back!"

But A. W. refused.

Days went by.

Nights went by.

Weeks went by, and A. W. still waited.

There was no sign of Bonzini.

And Kazoo, Texas, was as hot and dull as ever ...

. . . until one afternoon A. W. spotted a cloud of dust moving toward town.

He jumped up and cried, "Someone's coming to Kazoo!"